It was the end of Book Week.

Gus had to dress up as
a person from a book.

Adam was Jack

and Kim was Jill.

Jack

Jill

Hinda was Miss Muffet

and Seth was Robin Hood.

Miss Muffet

Robin Hood

Rob was a wizard

and Gus

was...

...a dragon!